Spaceports & Spidersilk

June 2024

Edited by
Marcie Lynn Tentchoff

Spaceports & Spidersilk
June 2024
Edited by Marcie Lynn Tentchoff

All rights reserved. No part of this publication may be reproduced or transmitted in any form or by any means, electronic or mechanical, including photocopying or recording or by any information storage and retrieval systems, without expressed written consent of the author and/or artists.

All characters herein are fictitious, and any resemblance between them and actual people is strictly coincidental.

Story and art copyrights owned by the respective authors and artists
Cover art "Phoenix" by Kat Heckenbach
Cover design by Laura Givens

First Printing, June 2024

Hiraeth Publishing
P.O. Box 1248
Tularosa, NM 88352
www.hiraethsffh.com
e-mail: hiraethsubs@yahoo.com

Visit www.hiraethsffh.com for science fiction, fantasy, horror, scifaiku, and more. While you are there, visit the Shop for books and more! **Support the small, independent press...**

Stories

12	Dust Bunny by Melva Gifford
19	Out of the Sands by Michael D. Winkle
39	The Gateway Bakery by Kevin Hopson
52	The Impossible Waterfall by Pamela Love
58	Teddy by Chris Farmer
70	Ants from Space by Bruno Lowagie
78	Blue Marble by Nicholas Samuel Stember

Poetry

18	How Some People Disappear by Jay Sturner
38	Aliens Visit the Youngest Brother by Lauren McBride
	Tanka by Denise Noe
51	Five Little Dragons by Lisa Timpf
69	what secrets by Lee Clark Zumpe
62	T-Rex by L. W. Lewis
77	Forward Control Thrusters by Katarzyna Lisińska

Illustrations

39	Biscuits and More by Vonnie Winslow Crist
78	Blue Marble by Vonnie Winslow Crist
89	Who's Who

SALE AT HIRAETH PUBLISHING!!!

BUY ALL THE BOOKS YOU WANT AND USE THIS 20% DISCOUNT CODE: BOOKS2024

GO TO OUR SHOP AT
WWW.HIRAETHSFFH.COM

NO MASKS, NO WAITING, AND WE NEVER CLOSE!

From the Editor

What is life?

I know, I know: asking impossible, philosophical questions is un-wise, especially on any day of the week that ends in the letter "y." Still, upon reading through the stories and poems in this issue, it is the question that first pops into my mind.

What is life? Or, more to the point, where is the line drawn between life and *un*-life?

I'm not talking about death, or at least not really. For something to be dead it must at one time have been alive. Same thing with *un*-death. Most of the ghosts, vampires, and zombies in popular stories were once living beings.

But how about things that never were alive, or, at least, never were *supposed* to be alive? What happens when inanimate objects are suddenly animate? When a teddy bear, for example, develops a personality, and a need to protect its owner? When a ball of dust, or even a mote of dust, turns out to be something more, with feelings, desires, and its own will?

And what about rights? If a thing, an un-alive thing, has personality, motivation, wants and needs, should it not have rights?

In fact, is it not just another form of life, beyond our understanding, but real none-the-less?

You will be (and probably already have been) hearing and reading things about AIs. Artificial intelligence has long been a juicy subject for science fiction stories and movies, but these days AIs, and questions and problems that arise because of them, are more and more in the news.

Un-alive. Alive. Tools. Beings.

In the end, I guess it doesn't mater what causes an un-alive thing to become closer to being alive. Maybe it comes about because of magic, or because of hopes and dreams, or maybe because of greater and more imaginative technologies.

What matters, after all, is less *how*, or *why* such a thing could happen, and more how we, as people, deal with something... no, some*one*, new, when it, or he, appears.

Welcome, readers, to the June 2024 issue of Spaceports & Spidersilk. Watch for the unexpected, whether by way of magic or technology. And consider, *consider,* that new thing as just another form of...

... life?

Mellie

The Adventures of a Teenage Vampire

Meet Mellie, an adolescent vampire, as she travels to Italy and New York to discover roots, make friends, and of course get into trouble. Fun adventures for the whole family.

https://www.hiraethsffh.com/product-page/mellie-the-adventures-of-a-teenage-vampire-by-debby-feo

Pyra and the Tektites
Aquarium in Space

Pyra, age thirteen, is running away from home in the Asteroid Belt because she's not doing well in school. Her parents want to send her to Mars for school, and she doesn't want to go. She sneaks aboard a cargo shuttle, and falls asleep in the hold. When she awakens, she finds herself in free-fall; the shuttle has been seized by the Tektites, a group of rebel pirates . . .

. . . and the adventures begin!

Order a copy of this thrilling adventure here:

https://www.hiraethsffh.com/product-page/pyra-and-the-tektites-1-by-tyree-campbell

Adopted Child
By Teri Santitoro

Imp, now 13, has awakened from stasis by MA, the ship's computer, to find that everyone else has been killed by a highly infectious disease. She is alone on the ship. But she is about to have visitors.

The *Greentown*, a salvage ship, has spotted a derelict and is about to board her for salvage rights. The crew is blissfully unaware of what happened to the people on the derelict. Soon enough they will find out...but will it be too late? And what of the girl who now controls the derelict?

To everyone involved, everything is new... and potentially lethal.

Ordering Link:

https://www.hiraethsffh.com/product-page/adopted-child-by-t-santitoro

Dust Bunny
Melva Gifford

Magen's mom pulled the chain cord that was inside the closet. "What a mess," She said as she stepped back into the bedroom.

Magen stood behind her mom, looking into the bare closet. The light from the room's East window brightened the room. Some of the brightness hit the closet's door. Magen saw particles of dust dance in the air and some faded shadows resting in the corner. "But nothing's in there, Mom."

"They're dust bunnies."

"Bunnies?" Magen's voice brightened.

"Not those kinds of bunnies," Mom said shaking her head. "I know I promised you could have a rabbit, once we find one; but these aren't the same. Dust bunnies are dirty. They're not pets. Just dust and dirt collected by static electricity."

"Static–"

"Never mind," her mom countered. "Stay here while I get the vacuum, ok?

As her mom walked away Mandy bent down for a closer look. The thing in the corner reminded her of the glob of dirt her mom would pull out of the vacuum after a day of cleaning. But instead of being knotted and heavy with dirt, this... shadowy thing was light, with strands of lint and thread intermixed with air. And every time her mom had gotten close, it moved. Was it alive?

"You're bunnies but not bunnies," she said to the shadow. Looking closer, she watched the shadow shift. The shadow had no real form, just a pile of... dirt and dust, just like her mom said. But it wasn't laying flat on the floor but was puffy.

"Are you scared?" Mandy asked, her voice turning gentle. "I won't hurt you; I promise."

She knelt. Reaching her hand out, the tan shadow backed away. It shifted in the slight breeze caused by Mandy's movements.

"It's ok," she said. "Are you hungry?"

She remembered a TV show where someone had fed a horse by pulling some leaves from a nearby bush. Mandy thought she'd try something similar. Picking up a small batch of stray lint, she slowly reached out. Surprisingly, the smaller glob of dust strands was gathered into the larger ones.

"You were hungry!" She said with a smile. "You would be easy to feed if you just eat dust..." She turned, hearing her mother coming up the steps. She turned back. "My mom doesn't like you guys," she whispered, noticing the smaller shadows near the largest. "But wait!" She said, eyes brightening. "Stay right there, I'll be back."

Jumping up from the floor, the air swished behind her. The dust bunny twirled in the air before landing once more on the wooden floor. Mandy ran over to her bed, pulled out a shoe box from beneath the mattress, and dumped out an old pair of Keds. Shoving the shoes under the bed, she hurried back to the closet. "No. No. You can't run away," she warned, seeing that the dust bunny was closer to the door. With gentle hands, she reached down and gently circled her fingers around the dust bunny. It was soft and prickly at the same time. Lifting it up, she put the bunny into the shoe box and closed the lid.

Her mom came through the door, dragging the vacuum. "Step back dear."

"Ok."

She watched as her mother vacuumed the closet until all the other dust bunnies were gone. Mandy clutched her shoe box close. "You're safe," she whiskered.

"What's that, dear?"

"Nothing, Mom."

Her mom began winding the cord up on the vacuum. "Ok, you stay here while I clean the hall, ok."

"Ok.' Closing the door behind her mom, Mandy opened her box. For a peak. The shadow shifted and then settled. "My very own bunny!" She said with a smile. "Even if you're just a dust bunny." She reached her hand in. The parts of the bunny that felt soft were areas of mostly lint and air. The prickly parts were specks of sticks, wires, and stuff.

"I'm not sure how I can pet you. But you do need a bath or at least a shower." Remembering the window cleaner her mom had left by her window. Mandy ran over to the window and got the spray bottle. She hurried back and with a single squirt, gave her bunny a shower. "I hope that'll help," she said, noting how the droplets of moisture were spotting the outside of the mound of fluff.

"Time for supper," her mom called out.

"Coming!" Mandy called out as she closed the box and put it on her bed. Hurrying downstairs, she was glad to have her secret pet.

Once she finished dinner, she ran upstairs to see if her new bunny needed feeding again. She closed the bedroom door and hurried over to the bed, She opened the box. The dust bunny was gone, leaving only a pile of dirt and threads.

"Where did you go?" she asked.

She sighed. "You ran away, even when I told you not to." She said with a frown. "You're not as fun as a real bunny." She thought a moment until she realized. It would be boring to live in a cage or a box. "I would want to escape too. Being free is better," she said. Satisfied now that the bunny, her dust bunny, was now free.

The Adventures of Colo Collins &
Tama Toledo in Space and Time
By Tyree Campbell

Out on their first date, high school seniors Colo Collins and Tama Toledo are invited aboard a spaceship and offered the chance to intervene in various events in the Universe. These events can range from stopping an asteroid from striking a planet to helping someone find her house keys. But there's a catch: both Colo and Tama have to agree that an intervention should be performed . . . and sometimes they'll have to perform the intervention themselves!

Ordering Link:

https://www.hiraethsffh.com/product-page/adventures-of-colo-collins-tama-toledo-in-space-and-time-by-tyree-campbell

How Some People Disappear
Jay Sturner

Found out
the hard way
that the dust mote
floating toward me
was a species of vampire
that doesn't bite
but feeds on you when inhaled,
either causing disease
or changing you into a vampire
just like itself.

Yes, I found out
through an online video
that some dust motes
aren't dust motes at all
but in fact a race of the undead.
At first I didn't believe it.
At first it seemed too strange.
But over several days and several nights
I shrank, painfully, into a
dust mote vampire.
Unfortunate, but true—so beware!
      For I just might
float on over
      to YOU!

Out of the Sands
Michael D. Winkle

Tawnja stared over the rust-red plain. The glassite window was so clear she kept expecting a cool night-breeze to blow in on her, bringing with it the sounds of silver locusts and ten-legged *banths*.

The door melted open. Tawnja always hoped John Carter or Northwest Smith would march boldly into her room someday and invite her to adventure, but it was just Oldrin.

"Watching for Tripods?" her brother asked as the door whopped back into existence behind him.

Tawnja glanced over her shoulder. She felt too good to scowl, but she did pout.

"Enjoying the sunset," she said. "It grows a little more purple every day. They pump more oxygen into the atmosphere, heat the land another degree or two, let loose more bacteria and lichen. Maybe we'll wake something from hibernation, under the sand or in the caves."

Oldrin snickered, his polyshirt flashing lavender and rose and aquamarine.

"Hibernation. *Please*, Tawnja, narc it. There's no life on Mars except what we brought with us."

Tawnja turned back to the window.

Oldrin winked on a light; the ghost of a reflection appeared in the glassite. Tawnja stared for a moment into her own dark eyes and face.

"How can you be so certain?" she asked. "They've been busy greening the Red Planet for a hundred years. No one's been searching for indigenous life as well as they might."

Oldrin dropped into his omnichair, which molded itself around him.

"It'd take a hundred more years to check every crevice and cave, even with every Rover and Sandroid working. And what's the most you can expect? Viruses, maybe. No little green men."

"Even that would be something," said Tawnja.

Oldrin waved his hand, and his selection screen blipped into view. He pressed nonexistent buttons.

"The seas of Mars turned out to be duststorms," he said. "The canals were optical illusions. Phobos and Deimos are just asteroids captured by the planet's gravity, not Martian space stations. The Face was a freak of geology. You can look out the window all you want, you won't see any four-armed warriors. Just sand, rocks and our Rovers."

A gray sphere enveloped Tawnja's brother. Cocooned in an interactive novel, he could not hear a retort if she had one to give.

She rose and stretched and left the Blue Room. She passed along the tubelike corridor, through the Yellow Room and on to her quarters. Her door dissolved, and she nodded to the north wall. The window, until now opaque, cleared. *Whop* went the door.

To the north an expanse of sand stretched to the distant wall of Edom Crater. The sky above was already black but dotted with a million stars. They twinkled. Once they shone as simple points as they would in deep space. To the west floated clouds, their bellies set ablaze by the sun, which had vanished below Lowell City's horizon.

An aerospace plane streaked past, amber-green lights blinking. In the sand, highlighted by the glow of the Domes, the tread- and ped-marks of Sandroids and Rovers formed abstract patterns.

She had always felt – no, she was *sure* – that she would clear the window some evening and see something else. That was why she had insisted on this bedroom since age five. Green Bluff, Illinois, *circa* 1926, mysteriously transplanted to Mars, perhaps. A birdlike creature calling "Preet! Preet!" An otterlike *Hross*, seeking the warm *handramit* of its birth.

But, like Oldrin said, there was nothing.

***

Where are you? . . . Where are you? . . . Where are you? . . .

Here.

Tawnja snorted. She had dozed off, her head cradled on her arms on the back of the couch. She had dreamt that at last there was something. She couldn't help looking out the window as she rose.

Siliceous particles glinted in the light of the main Domes. There was a bump in the sand, growing slowly, moving. It reminded her of holos she'd seen of earthly gophers in dirt.

She blinked at the window for 20x magnification. There *was* something. Glassy flecks trickled down the front and sides of the bump, a sparkling avalanche in miniature. At the base, on both the right and left, something stirred the sand. The image came to Tawnja of a newly-hatched sea-turtle digging out of a nest.

However, there were no seas on Mars, and no turtles.

Tawnja exhaled loudly. She touched her fingertip to the intercom, concentrating on the Command Center code. Then she yanked her hand away.

This was not for C.C. Not yet. It was Tawnja who believed in Martians, Tawnja who pestered Dr. Muraki and Major DeWeese for bio-reports. This was Tawnja Nagomi's discovery.

***

The Evac station accepted her ID card; curfew for her age group was not for thirty minutes. It would let her back in at any time, of course, but it would take note if she broke curfew.

Excrepods! No one will care about that! she thought.

She seized the grip-bar above the E-suit with her wiry brown hands and swung forward. She thrust her legs into the twin openings below then she plunged her arms into the cold fluicine sleeves. She pulled the helmet down and heard the *shlupp* as the seams of the suit joined.

The Evac hatch closed behind her. A hiss filled her ears as her suit inflated. The hiss continued as the airlock depressurized.

There were no quiet melt-doors facing the raw Martian atmosphere. The huge airlock door slid aside with a seismic rumble. Tawnja gulped. Here was the descending titanium apron, the narrow glassy plaza, and beyond, the sand – the sand from which *something* emerged, even now.

Wind whipped across the opening, audible even through the background-voices of the main com-channel. Tawnja focused on the radio controls and made the eye motions necessary to shut off the sound.

She blinked several times and rolled her eyes; too many retinal codes gave her a headache. And she could not afford to hesitate. What if the Martian scuttled off or disappeared back into the sand? She bit her lip and clumped down the titanium apron.

***

Tawnja worked her way around the color-domes to the north side of the settlement. She used the silica walks when possible, and when she had to wade through the sand she consulted her sonilyzer to pick out the sturdiest paths.

The sands of Mars were deep here. Anything could be buried down there, beyond the reach of the last century's surveys.

She displayed the read-out on the inside of her helmet. Rock lumps showed green beneath the orange grid that represented the surface. Nothing moved.

She listened to the distant crunch of her boots and the low rush of her respiration.

The images she received were blurry; could she be *sure* those were boulders, and not Martians, rolled up like lungfish?

"Maybe I can ask this one," she whispered.

She touched the manual control buttons on her right sleeve to turn on her head lamps. She used a soft, lemon-yellow light at first, just strong enough to let her pick her way. She didn't want to attract attention from the Domes, and she didn't want to startle the Martian.

Startle the Martian . . . What a thought.

There – just ahead – her bedroom window was to port; she had seen it right around here.

Tawnja heard a clattering. *What was that?* she thought, then, *Oh.*

It was her teeth clicking together. She upped her scan-light by several candlepower. A rust-red pool rippled over the landscape.

A chill crept along her spine; it was not due to the frigid Martian night. Her legs wobbled as if she had been marching for hours.

"Cryon out, Tawnja," she whispered. "This is what you've always wanted. This is what you've dreamed about. *Expected*, even."

The circle of light passed over a half-moon of darkness. A pit. A meteorite crater?

No. She stepped up and knelt by the pit. Sand and pebbles had been pushed aside, not blown out. There were furrows in the silica dust, like finger scratches; the first strong wind would erase them.

She thought of her suit's camera. She started recording. She wondered about narrating.

"This – this is Tawnja Nagomi. Terradate – uh – 17 Aug, 2251. The Martian emerged from the sand. Here."

She sounded like she was ready to puke. She shut up for now.

Her light revealed a trail – a meter-wide drag mark with indecipherable prints on either side of the central furrow. She followed it.

***

There it was ahead, a gray mass in the diffuse yellow of her light. It had made good progress – some hundreds of meters – in the time it took Tawnja to get here.

She stopped and watched it creep across the sand. She heard a bass drum pounding in her ears and an asthmatic wheeze in her helmet – her heart and her breath.

You'll hyper, she told herself. *Think alpha waves.*

She concentrated on calming herself, and slowly the Martian crawled away. It looked rather like a lobster from behind, only bristly.

"'Kay," said Tawnja aloud. "I've gravved myself. Now – contact."

She trudged forward. Her helmet lights engulfed the Martian. It gave no indication that it noticed. Did it even have eyes?

She circled to the right and came up parallel to it. The Martian looked a bit like a huge praying mantis, only with a thicker body and thicker legs. It possessed six limbs; it crept along on all of them at the moment, but the first two appeared to end in long, articulated fingers.

Tawnja blinked on the speaker of her suit.

"Ahem!" she called into the thin Martian air. "Uh – Mr. Martian . . ."

She winced. The holo she recorded would make her famous, but it would also make her look retarded.

The Martian still seemed oblivious to her presence. It crawled toward the Edom Crater wall. Tawnja bit her lip again. She hopped and ran and planted herself directly in its path. It kept coming.

"The Martian is approximately three meters in length," she said nervously. "Its general outline is insectile, an effect enhanced by its posture and its six limbs . . . Uh . . . It is covered with bristly hair of a grayish-green color."

The Martian crept on. It was five meters away, then four. Tawnja gulped so loudly she knew the audio recorded it.

"Its head – its head – is insectile, too. Wide, circular eyes, antennae, but instead of mandibles it possesses a birdlike beak. It –"

She gasped. Seams opened across the Martian's softball-sized eyes. Lids or nictating membranes slid back to reveal glassy orbs of lavender blue. Maybe that was why it had not noticed her – its eyes had been closed.

The front half of the Martian bent back – or up. Now its posture was very much that of a mantis. Its long abdomen remained parallel to the ground, supported by four legs, but its "chest" was vertical, and its "arms" hung from well developed shoulders. Its head bobbed several centimeters higher than Tawnja's.

"Uh – Hunnh – Hujja – " came a sound. The Martian, talking? No, Tawnja was gibbering. She clenched her teeth and raised one gloved hand in the (supposedly) universal sign for peace.

"I know you don't understand my language," she said, "but I greet you in the name of all my – er – species."

The Martian stopped. Its wide eyes appeared to focus on her faceplate. It winced – at least, its eyelids closed partially – and Tawnja lowered the intensity of her lights to a ghostly white.

The girl touched her hand to the lamp on the side of her helmet.

"We use technology. These lights – this suit – you see that they're artificial, don't you?"

The mantislike creature moved its head to follow her hand but otherwise stood statue-still. For the first time Tawnja felt doubt. Maybe this being was not intelligent – merely an animal. If so, she hoped it was not a predator like the insect it resembled.

She spoke on because she could think of nothing else to do.

"We flew here from the third planet. We come in peace." She pointed to the horizon. "We come from Earth. The blue one."

The Martian looked up, but not toward the horizon. It kept its eyes on her hand. Tawnja thought of her old dog Rufe, who would just watch her finger when she'd point at his ball or rubber bone and say "Fetch!" Maybe it *was* only an animal.

Then the Martian raised its own hand.

Tawnja studied its forelimb even as her stomach flipped in joy and nervousness. It had more joints than a human arm, ending in a triangular palm that branched out into seven stringbean-looking digits.

"You are intelligent," whispered Tawnja. "Or are you just imitating me? . . . Well, imitation must count for *something*."

The Martian lowered its arm. It extended its hand exactly as a human would when greeting someone. The girl gasped.

"Maybe some things *are* universal," she said aloud.

She extended her own hand, its fluicine-sheaved fingers like so many sausages. The Martian's spidery phalanges closed over it. Then –

The Martian's arm jerked. There was a hiss on her audio pickup and a sharp sting in the palm of her hand.

"Hey!" yelled Tawnja. Then –

***

She remembered the shallow sea of Ull-*click*-Yat, and the deep violet sunsets, and the beetlelike Vull-thups in the hills. She recalled Venus with her moon and green oceans. She recalled Ssa-lig, the planet between Mars and Jupiter, and she knew of the third planet, Venus' twin, with its unique, primitive life-forms.

She remembered the Catastrophe as well, which the Martians never quite understood, when the fifth planet burst asunder and showered its neighbors with meteorites. The impacts split the crust of the not-yet-Red Planet, burned off her atmosphere and boiled away her seas. Most of the insectic inhabitants died, but a few thousand of the most knowledgeable – those Wise Ones part philosopher, part scientist and part wizard – developed a way to preserve themselves – or, should that fail, at least their memories.

They treated their bodies to become like rock, and had themselves buried by Vullthup drones, and like rock they would remain until the atmosphere thickened and the rains returned and life could exist on Mars again.

***

We reclaimed oxygen from the rusted sands, thought Tawnja dimly. *We diverted ice comets so that they'd steam across the skies. We released algae and bacteria to create a primitive eco-system.*

She arrested her train of thought. Where was she? More importantly, where was the Martian?

She opened her eyes and stared up. Clouds scudded before the night wind. Grains of sand skittered across her faceplate. She was still outside.

Her hand – she lifted it, and it thunked clumsily against her helmet as if her arm were asleep. She could not detect a puncture in her glove, but the E-suit would have automatically sealed any rupture.

The Martian, then. Where was it?

She sat up and scanned the area. She had not moved or been moved while she lay unconscious. She blinked on and punched on motion-sensors, heat-scanners, UV detectors – nothing.

She looked down dejectedly then gasped. The Martian lay at her feet, no more than a shell, an empty exoskeleton. Its beaked head might have rested on the crater floor a million years.

Tawnja flexed her right hand. Her palm itched.

They wanted to preserve their bodies – or, at least, their memories, she told herself.

She thought of Earth. An image filled her mind of the Earth *they* knew: an ocean-planet filled with nightmarish life-forms – creatures as strange to Tawnja as the Martians themselves. *Was* that Earth? She saw no dinosaurs, pterodactyls, ammonites –

Wait – one creature she had seen before. A thing like a ribcage, with tentacles sprouting from the back, each of which ended in a mouth. It was the weirdest animal she had ever heard of, and it was native to Earth.

Or, rather, it had been. The ribcage-creature and other bizarre life-forms had been found in the Burgess shale, somewhere in Canada. But they died out five hundred and fifty million years ago, if she remembered her paleontology! Over half a billion years! Was the Martian *that* old? No wonder it crumbled to dust!

An orange light blinked below her right eye. A soft beep accompanied it. Past curfew. A few minutes more and they would search for her.

She studied the landscape. For an instant she saw soil, cycad-like trees, insects with bird-beaks. She shook her head within her helmet.

Better get back, she thought.

She knelt and lifted Arri-*click's* skull carefully. The exobiologists would drool over it. Arri-*click*, a scientist himself, would not have minded.

? – That's his name! she thought in amazement.

***

She hiked toward Theta entrance, as it was closest. A contact signal flashed in her helmet. She ignored it.

The clouds hung heavy tonight. A pale mist danced in the lights of the highest Domes. Tiny white flakes whipped past her faceplate.

The mistiness was rain. It was thin, and it froze long before it reached the ground, but it was rain.

Tawnja envisioned the hibernating Martians, thousands of them, buried all over the planet, waiting for the rain. More would awaken; some would inject their memories into other colonists; one or two might even recover from their billion-year sleep. But Tawnja had greeted the first Martian. No one could take that from her.

"I, Tawnja Nagomi, have just participated in the most important encounter in human history," she announced to the universe. "We will learn all there is to be learned about a truly alien civilization. And best of all, Oldrin will have to eat his words!"

She realized the camera, being sound activated, had dutifully recorded her last statement. She could edit –

She laughed and hopped a meter-wide fissure in the brick-red rock. Far be it from her to tamper with history. Let it stand.

***

A thousand years later, children human and Martian still laughed at Tawnja's brother Oldrin.

Aliens, Magic, and Monsters
By Lauren McBride

Fun to read. Fun to write. *Aliens, Magic, and Monsters* features poems set in the unlimited and imaginative realm of science fiction, fantasy, and horror. The poems were chosen to showcase over twenty poetic forms from acrostiku to zip, from strict rhyme to free verse, and much more in between. There are guidelines included on how to write each type of poem. Try a sci(na)ku. At only six words, it's sure to interest even the youngest readers.

Type: Juvenile and Young Adult Poetry Manual
Ordering links:
Print: https://www.hiraethsffh.com/product-page/aliens-magic-and-monsters-by-lauren-mcbride

ePub: https://www.hiraethsffh.com/product-page/aliens-magic-and-monsters-by-lauren-mcbride-2

PDF: https://www.hiraethsffh.com/product-page/aliens-magic-and-monsters-by-lauren-mcbride-1

The Caves of Titan
By Debby Feo

Students at the Galileo Interplanetary School explore new-found caves on Titan, where they encounter the Cenote People and learn to get along with them—and with each other, as they continue to grow and learn in a diverse student body. Still, there are conflicts to resolve . . . and some of them might put an end to the school!

Ordering link:

Print Edition ($10.00):
https://www.hiraethsffh.com/product-page/caves-of-titan-by-debby-feo

Aliens Visit the Youngest Brother
Lauren McBride

Honest!
And then they asked
if I could fold into
my flat self to ride up with them
to their 2-D space ship, which they did, and
then left, and that's why you won't get
to meet them yet . . . What? You
don't believe me?
Honest!

speed of light
faster!
in space
no stop signs
not even yields

    Denise Noe

The Gateway Bakery
Kevin Hopson

Biscuits and More by Vonnie Winslow Crist

"Cameron," my father shouted.

I turned to him, his hazel eyes meeting my gaze. My father was a stocky man with cropped brown hair, and he stood behind the counter of the bakery with a plate in each hand.

"Yeah?" I said.

"Two pieces of carrot cake for table five."

I nodded and approached him. My father rested the plates on the counter and pivoted, putting his back to me as he worked on other orders. He owned the bakery. And even though I was only thirteen, I would sometimes help out, especially on busy days like this one.

As I grasped the plates and headed toward the table, a whiff of cinnamon and toasted pecans tugged at my nostrils. I wasn't a huge fan of carrot cake, but I had to admit that the aroma was pleasing. My favorite part was the velvety cream cheese frosting. Sometimes I would eat the frosting and leave the cake for my little sister, but she didn't appreciate that. Nor did my father.

Two older men eyed me as I neared their table. Mr. Spencer was a balding man with patches of gray hair, while Mr. Harrington had dark, bushy eyebrows and a protruding nose.

"Here you go," I said, resting the plates in front of them.

"Thank you, Cameron," Mr. Spencer replied.

Mr. Harrington pursed his lips but nodded his approval.

"I haven't seen you in a few days," I said to Mr. Harrington.

"Funny story," Mr. Spencer said. "I hadn't seen him either. Not since he left for Nevilia. I thought he was stuck there, so I ate a piece of your father's magical carrot cake and paid him a visit. When I found him, he was having the time of his life. He wasn't stuck there. He just didn't want to come back." Mr. Spencer couldn't help but chuckle.

"True enough," Mr. Harrington said. "But I came back, didn't I?"

Mr. Spencer grinned. "Only after a little persuading."

"Does that mean you're heading back to Nevilia now?" I asked.

Mr. Harrington shook his head. "No. Just regular carrot cake for us today. Maybe next week, though."

All of my father's desserts came in two varieties. One with normal ingredients, and one with magical ingredients. The magical desserts transported people to another world, so those were more expensive.

For example, the carrot cake sent people to Nevilia. The pecan pie opened a door to Suanus. And the cinnamon rolls created a gateway to Eleshan.

However, in order to get back home, a person had to eat a piece of that same magical dessert. That's why my father insisted that customers pack away a large piece of their dessert before eating it. Because it only took one bite to send them on their way. On occasion, customers would get stuck in another world, and friends or family would have to go and retrieve them.

Something brushed against my leg, snapping me from my thoughts. I looked down, and Haru stared back at me. She was a black and white cat that we owned. I watched as she moseyed over to an empty table. Then my eyes bulged. A leftover piece of cinnamon roll lay on the floor, and Haru swiftly snatched it up with her mouth.

"No," I shouted.

By the time I reached her, Haru had already swallowed the piece of food, her body disappearing right in front of me. I ran to the counter as my heart pounded up into my throat.

"Dad!"

He spun around to face me. "What is it?"

"It's Haru. She ate a piece of your magical roll and vanished."

My father's eyes narrowed. "Are you sure?"

"Yes, I'm sure."

"She could have taken off. You know how she is. She's here one second and gone the next."

I vehemently shook my head. "She didn't take off. I witnessed the entire thing, and I didn't take my eyes off of her. She's been transported to Eleshan."

My father let out a frustrated breath. "What have I told you about bringing Haru to the bakery? I was afraid something like this might happen."

"Are you really going to lecture me at a time like this?"

"Alright," he said, raising a dismissive hand at me. "Take a breath and calm down. We'll figure this out."

"I have to go after her," I barked.

"That's out of the question. Someone else can retrieve her. Or I can go once the bakery closes."

"It will be too late by then. She could get lost, and we'll never be able to find her."

"Cameron," he said, keeping a steady tone. "She'll be fine. You just need to be patient."

"Hey, boss." One of my father's co-workers stood in the doorway to the kitchen.

My father turned to him. "What is it, Gabriel?"

"I need help with one of the flour bags. It will only take a minute."

"Sure. I'll be right there." My father eyed me again. "It's going to be okay, Cameron. Haru is a hardy cat. If it makes you feel any better, I'll see if I can close up early. In the meantime, I need you to bring this order to table three."

I huffed and watched as my father disappeared into the kitchen. I went to pick up the plate, and that's when I noticed the cinnamon roll resting on top of it. I couldn't tell if it was a magical one or not. All of them looked the same to me. But I grasped it, nonetheless.

I broke off a small piece, stuffing the rest of it into the pocket of my pants. Then I raised the roll to my mouth and bit into the flaky crust. A mix of cinnamon, sugar, and butter hit my taste buds. As much as I wanted to savor the taste, I was on a mission, so I quickly chewed and swallowed.

The bakery immediately vanished, and I found myself somewhere else. Trees surrounded me. With the exception of a few pines, most of the trees were bare, and there was a dirt road at my feet. It looked as if it cut through the middle of the forest. The damp and chilly air weighed on me, and my body protested with a shiver.

I wish I'd brought a jacket, but I hadn't given much thought to my actions. I just wanted to find Haru and get back before my father noticed I was missing.

A noise stole my attention. It was a cat's meow, and it came from above. I titled my head back and peered up into the tree. Haru was perched on a branch about halfway up.

"Oh, Haru," I muttered to myself. "What have you gotten yourself into?"

Then came another sound. The snapping of a twig caused me to flinch. A figure appeared between two trees, and I took a step back.

"Sorry," the boy said. "I didn't mean to sneak up on you."

He was a lanky boy. A tad taller than me, and maybe a little older as well. He had black, curly locks and brown eyes.

"Is that your cat?" he asked, glancing toward the sky.

I couldn't muster a response.

"I'm afraid it's my fault," the boy said. "The cat was so startled when it saw me that it ran up the tree." He hesitated. "By the way, my name is Daniel."

I swallowed, trying to choke down my anxiety. "Cameron," I replied.

"It's nice to meet you, Cameron. So, is that your cat?"

I nodded.

"Again, I apologize for frightening him. Or is it a her."

"Her name is Haru."

Daniel bobbed his head. "Fortunately, I may be able to help."

I raised an eyebrow. "Are you a really good climber?"

A chuckle escaped Daniel's lips. "Hardly. But I do have another gift."

"And what's that?"

"It's probably best if I showed you."

Daniel sidled up to me and eyed Haru.

"Hi, Haru," he said. "I'm going to get you down. How does that sound?"

Haru could only meow in response. I

stared at her, my eyes going wide at the sight. Haru started hovering above the branch. Then she slowly descended, eventually making her way into my outstretched arms. I hugged her, pressing her against my chest and rubbing my chin over her soft fur.

"How did you do that?" I asked.

"I can move things with my mind," Daniel answered. "Ever since I can remember." He paused. "But it looks like I'm not the only one who possesses magic."

My brow furrowed. "What do you mean?"

"The way you and Haru just appeared out of nowhere. Are you portal jumpers?"

I debated whether to tell Daniel the truth.

"Sort of," I finally said. "But not because of any magic of our own. My father is a baker, and his desserts can transport people between worlds."

"Interesting. Where are you from?"

"A place called Ballinreen. Ever heard of it?"

"Can't say that I have," Daniel replied. He pondered for a moment. "Is it a nice place?"

"Of course. It's my home, and I love it there."

Daniel nodded. "It sounds like a place I'd like to visit."

I couldn't tell if he was hinting at something, or if he was just trying to be nice.

"I live by myself," Daniel said. "My parents died a couple of years ago. But I manage to get by on my own."

I couldn't imagine living on my own, especially at my age.

"Where do you live?" I asked.

"In the nearby town. A place called Eastgal."

I took a deep breath as I mulled things over. "Would you like to come back with us?"

Daniel's lips stretched into a grin. "Really?"

I realized I was being impulsive, but it was too late to rescind my offer. "Yeah. Why not?"

"What do I have to do?"

I held Haru in one hand and slid my free hand into the pocket of my pants. Then I pulled the remaining cinnamon roll from it.

"Take some of this," I said. "But don't eat it until I say so."

He broke off a big chunk of the roll. "What is it?"

"A sweet roll. But my hands are full, so maybe you can give Haru a piece of yours."

Daniel nodded. He tore off a piece of his roll and held it up to Haru's mouth. She grasped it with her teeth and chewed.

"Now it's our turn," I said.

I lifted the roll to my mouth and took a bite, depositing the rest of it in my pocket. Then Daniel munched on a piece of his own, his eyes going wide with apparent delight.

The warmth of the bakery was the first thing I felt upon my return. When I inspected my surroundings, I noticed that all of the customers' eyes were on me. Or maybe they were on Daniel. He stood beside me, while Haru was cradled in my arms.

My father walked out from behind the counter. "Cameron! I can't believe you did that."

I had nothing to say in my defense. Nothing that would justify my actions, at least. My shoulders slumped in embarrassment.

"I'm sorry, Dad," I finally said. "But I managed to retrieve Haru. Thanks to Daniel here."

My father glimpsed Daniel before meeting my gaze again. "You know we're not supposed to bring back people from other worlds."

"But Daniel wanted to visit," I said. "And he doesn't have any family back home."

The scowl on my father's face quickly faded. "I'm sorry to hear that," he said to Daniel, looking the boy up and down. "How old are you, young man?"

"Fourteen, sir."

"And you've been living on your own?"

Daniel nodded. "Yes, sir. My parents died from sickness when I was twelve. I have no siblings or other living relatives."

My father pursed his lips.

A thud caused me to look away. An empty glass at a nearby table had fallen on its side, and it rolled toward the edge of the table. I recognized the woman sitting there. It was Ms. Bennett. She reached out to grasp the glass but couldn't catch it in time. The glass tumbled over the side, falling toward the floor.

Then something amazing happened. The glass stopped in midair, hovering beside the table. The glass slowly made its way back to the table, coming to a rest in front of Ms. Bennett. Her eyes bulged at the sight.

"How—" My father's mouth hung agape.

"It's a gift of mine," Daniel said. "Moving objects with my mind. It comes in handy, especially with construction projects. Some things are too heavy for people to lift. Or too high for them to reach. It's how I earn my keep and support myself."

A thought came to me.

"He could help with the bakery," I blurted out. I glanced at Daniel. "If he chooses to stay."

"I would like that," Daniel replied. "There isn't much for me to go back to, so I wouldn't mind sticking around. For a short time, at least."

My father grunted. "I suppose I could use your help. You would need a place to stay, though."

Daniel and I glimpsed one another.

"I have a room above the bakery," my father said. "It's not much, but you're welcome to stay there. And you can help yourself to anything in the bakery. All in exchange for your assistance."

Daniel offered a toothy smile. "It's a deal, sir." He extended his hand, and my father shook it.

My father shifted his gaze to me and took a step forward. "As for you, Cameron. You owe Ms. Bennett an apology for the cinnamon roll you stole."

I was tempted to argue but held my tongue. "Of course," I finally said. "I'm sorry, Ms. Bennett."

"It's okay, dear," she said.

My father rested a hand on my shoulder and grinned. "But I'm glad you and Haru made it back safely. And that we have a new friend in Daniel here."

I smiled. "Me, too, Dad."

Five Little Dragons
Lisa Timpf

Five little dragons leave the nest;
One speeds off to perform a quest.

Four little dragons soaring higher
One gets burned when he plays with fire.

Three little dragons revel in flight
One peels off to confront a knight.

Two little dragons admire their reflection.
One gets obsessed with his own perfection.

One little dragon, last one left,
By the name of Paul, flies alone, bereft.

On a balmy night, when he feels the pull,
Of the rising tide, and the moon is full

With a fiery hiss and a haunting sigh
Paul will flap and trace a trail 'cross the sky.

Scientists call it a fireball.
The rest of us know that it's only Paul.

The Impossible Waterfall
Pamela Love

After taking a photo of Mom and me standing beside the spaceship we'd flown here, Dr. Bakisto asked, "What do you think of this waterfall world?"

"You discovered a waterfall?" I asked. Mom's friend Arturo Bakisto is a famous explorer—he found this planet. Mom's a geologist, so when he invited her here to help set up a research station, I begged to come along so I could meet him. She agreed, if I promised to keep up with my studies.

Now Mom looked puzzled. "No, Casey, he couldn't have. My scans show no liquid water on Planet W88L2, Arturo. The atmosphere is too thin." She gestured to the rocky, desert ground, free of plants, dirt, or even sand.

Dr. Bakisto laughed. "Ah, it is difficult to understand me through my space helmet." He tapped his face plate. "Also because of my accent, perhaps. On my home world they speak Esperanto, not English. I said this world is *wonderful*.

"But I did find where a waterfall *was*. It is no longer there, but on a cliff not far from here you can see where water cut a path across the rock. That is called..." He tapped his foot. "In Esperanto it is *erozio*. The English word is very similar—"

"Erosion?" I guessed.

He nodded. "That is correct. I will show it to you and your mother."

"Today?" I asked, almost bouncing with excitement. I want to be an explorer too, and this was my first time off Earth. A chance to scout out a planet with Dr. Bakisto was something I'd dreamed of since I was six.

But Mom shook her head. "First things first." Which meant all of us had to start building the research station by assembling the prefab rooms we'd brought. Setting up the plumbing would take longer, but was even more important. People can't live without water, so we'd brought plenty. We also had to recycle what we could, and conserve every drop. It could be days, even weeks, before we had spare time for a side trip. I groaned.

Dr. Bakisto picked up one end of a crate full of pipes. "So much exploration must be done with lab equipment, Casey. There are things on this planet we need a, what is the word, *microscope* to see. Small things can be very important."

That made me feel even worse. Did my hero think I was too immature to be here? I sighed and picked up the other end of his crate.

***

The next morning, Mom and I were eating breakfast on our spaceship when her comm link buzzed. "Help! Quick! I found a waterfall

—" Then it cut off, but not before we heard a splash!

She hit the call return button, but it didn't connect. "Suit up, Casey. I might need your help."

"But we don't know where the waterfall is." Hoping Dr. Bakisto wasn't hurt, I grabbed our first aid kit just in case.

"I'm guessing it's near the remains of the one he told us about yesterday. Where there was water once, it's more likely there's water still." I slipped into my suit while she checked a map. "Looks like the closest ridge is about five kilometers due south of here. Let's go."

The rover's so loud I understood for the first time why it's nicknamed the "roarer". But it was fast, and soon we reached a chain of rocky hills. As we approached, I pointed to a channel running down the side of the largest one. Water must have carved it eons ago. "There's the old waterfall."

Switching on the rover's spotlight, I swept it over the area, as Mom drove slowly past. There was no sign of her colleague or his rover.

"Now what?" I asked, starting to sweat with nervousness. "How can we find a secret waterfall on a desert planet?"

She frowned. "Arturo *must* be nearby. There's water at the polar regions, but that's frozen and too distant."

Suddenly I leaned forward. "Isn't that a cave?" Mom braked.

Half-hidden behind a huge, layered rock was a cave mouth. We climbed out of the rover and shone our flashlights inside. "Arturo!" Mom shouted.

"Turo...Turo..." came a faint echo.

"Mom, I've read there might be liquid water underground on planets even when there's none above. Maybe the waterfall is through there."

I took a step closer to the entrance, but Mom held up a hand to stop me. "Yes, but exploring caves can be very risky, and there's no evidence Arturo's inside."

"We have to do something!" I said, waving my arms in frustration.

She stomped her foot, which surprised me. Mom almost never shows when she's angry. "Why did he go out alone? You worked so hard yesterday that we decided to reward you with a surprise trip here this morning. That's what I thought he was calling about."

"Wait a second." Closing my eyes, I thought hard. "Mom, please play his message again."

"Help! Quick! I found waterfall—" *Splash.*

Mom started to pace. "Forget the waterfall —where did he find enough liquid water on this world to splash?"

My heartbeat accelerated. "I think we brought it. We didn't hear all of his message. He didn't say he found *a* waterfall. What if he was saying he found water *falling?*"

Mom gasped. "The plumbing!"

We raced back over the rocky terrain. Inside the lab, we found Dr. Bakisto desperately clutching where two pipes were joined, thin streams of water flowing from under his gloves. His comm link lay at his feet where it had slipped out of his hands and landed in a big puddle, cracking its screen.

Mom and I went into action—well, mostly Mom. But I helped by hanging onto another pipe which was also dripping badly. Working together, we were able to shut off the water circulation. (Dr. Bakisto didn't dare let go of the pipes to turn off that valve himself. Too much water would have been lost.)

It turned out Dr. Bakisto had used some screws from his own toolkit which didn't fit the pipes properly. He put his face in his hands. "Yesterday I said small things are important. If only I had checked the pipes then."

"But you checked them this morning," Mom said, patting him on the shoulder. "If you hadn't, we might have had to postpone starting the research station."

"Yes, you came back in time. But why did you leave when I called?" Dr. Bakisto asked. "I shouted when I heard the rover."

Mom and I took turns explaining. Dr. Bakisto nodded. "I am sorry. I wanted to say I found a flood—*inundo* in Esperanto—but I did not remember the English word. So I *did* start to say 'water falling in the lab' but you see my broken comm link." He leaned back and laughed. "It did feel like I was holding back Niagara Falls."

I asked, "Is there enough time for us to go out again today? I'd love to get a better look at the waterfall erosion on that cliff, and the cave, too."

"Cave?" Looking eager, Dr. Bakisto sat up straight. "What cave?"

"Casey found one." Mom said with pride.

My hero gave me a high five. "Good work, young explorer. Future maps will call it "Casey's Cave."

Teddy
Chris Farmer

Sir Arthur 'Teddy' Tedsworth sat at the edge of the long concrete piling tube that he and Amira had called their home for the past two weeks. Winds blew in from the south, bringing with it a cold chill that swept through the downtown streets of the city, stirring up dust and debris. Teddy tightened his grip on his steel sword and took a deep breath. It wouldn't be long until dawn, when the rising sun sent marauders, scavengers and people that would harm Amira back in to their own dark places, deep in the bowels of the city. He blinked, trying to keep his one good eye focused on the corner of the street. He barely stifled a yawn and his mind started to wander, as it did more and more these days.

He was getting on in his years now. He'd been with Amira for as long as he could remember, doing what all good teddy bears did: protecting her from whatever scared her. First, he protected her from terrifying beasts that hid in the shadows under her bed, creepy crawlies that crept out from under her pillow, and ajar wardrobe doors behind which creepy clowns, ghastly ghosts and dreadful demons lurked, waiting to pounce on an asleep Amira. Teddy had even endured a month-long feud with a reoccurring nightmare in which a black octopus sought to drag Amira into the swirling and churning waters below, but he'd prevailed. Victorious.

And then the war came.

For a few months, Amira and her family had survived in their residential block just south of the city center. But when the military jets flew over before the crack of dawn, dropping bombs indiscriminate across the city, when Amira's mother and father didn't surface from the rubble, Amira set out into the unknown world, scared, bloodied, cut and bruised, but not alone. Teddy was wrapped in her arms, more determined than ever to keep her safe.

And that was when the hard work really started, the work that aged Teddy, that injured and wounded him, that took his eye and ripped his delicate fabric. The things he had since done to protect Amira made scary octopuses and creepy crawlies pale in comparison.

It was winter now, many months since her mother and father had been buried beneath the remains of their home. The red jumper and black trousers were all she had. If the chattering of her teeth didn't wake her, the hubbub of the war-torn city did. And though Amira's thoughts had been darkened by the death and misery she had seen; she was able to rest in some comfort knowing that she still had Teddy.

Teddy jolted awake. Something had moved in the distance. His beady eye darted to the end of the street, which led off towards one of the main streets through the city. He groaned as he rose to his feet, his back stiff but the grip on his steel sword firm.

'Halt,' Teddy said. The man froze as he stepped into the narrow backstreet. He looked around to see from where the voice had come, fear suddenly upon him. 'Turn back!'

'Who's there?' The man's spoke with a lisp, some of his front teeth missing.

Teddy recognized people like him: he'd been protecting Amira from them for months. The problem was, they were much more dangerous than the creatures that lurked behind ajar wardrobe doors. Monsters scared a lot easier than humans, and humans are a lot more dangerous than monsters. Indeed, it was against a human that he had lost his first fight, and in that fight, he had suffered more than just a defeat: he lost his eye too. As he had lay there, barely able to do more than hold the whole in his fabric where his eye had been, panic had gripped him as he feared for Amira, the girl he had sworn to himself to protect, but the woman had left them alone. Afterwards, Amira tied a black bandanna around his head to cover the exposed fluff and thread.

Teddy hopped down from the pipe and ran behind the nearest pile of something that may have been a house or apartment complex. Teddy clamped his worn golden hand around his sword and leapt towards the man, twisting in mid-air to strike the head. Landing on the floor behind the man, Teddy turned. Ready.

"Who's there?" The man span on the spot, one hand holding his bloody temple, eyes searching to find whatever had hit him. He stumbled into a pool of moonlight. Teddy saw the man's face for the first time: greasy brown hair hung down in front of wild, brown eyes. His beard was ragged, caked with dirt and scraps of food, and his face bore many cuts, scrapes and scars. The man turned again, twisting on the spot to find his assailant.

From the pipe, Amira groaned in her sleep. Teddy looked round. She'd be awake soon and Teddy would do anything to protect her -- even from the sight of the scary man.

Bringing his gaze back, Teddy lunged at the man. Sword glistening in the silver moonlight, Teddy forced the sword into the back of the man's right calf. Before the man could react, Teddy quick as a flash pulled the sword away and slashed up, between the man's legs. The man roared, twisting away from Teddy. Teddy stepped backwards, ready to strike a fourth time but stopped.

The man had seen him.

He rushed towards Teddy, arms outstretched. Teddy leapt at the man's face, lunging with his sword. The man ducked the sword and grabbed Teddy. Having expected to grab something heavier, perhaps a small bratty child, the man stumbled and they both fell to the dusty ground. Seeing the advantage, Teddy gripped his sword and pushed it into the man's neck, pushing harder until it drew blood.

"I'll let you walk out of here with your life if you never come back. Got it?" Teddy snarled.

The man's eyes crossed as he looked at the steel blade, before turning back to Teddy's face. A frown creased his forehead. He couldn't believe what he was seeing. His eyes glanced from Teddy's covered eye to the scar on his cheek, then fell on Teddy's one remaining eye. *A teddy bear was attacking him?*

Teddy held the man's gaze. "Got it?"

Fear gripped Teddy and hid heart pounded in his throat. He had to send the man on his way quickly. They'd made too much noise--Amira was bound to have heard them. Teddy looked at the man's face.

He wasn't scared.

From the concrete tube came a gentle voice. "Teddy?"

Amira had awoken.

Teddy turned to look at her, his eyes softening as his looked. He lifted the sword away for just a second...

The man took his chance.

He gripped Teddy's arms and flung him against the nearest wall. Teddy hit the wall and fell several feet onto a pile of mortar and rubble. Stars formed in his mind. He shook his head to clear them and tried to stand up, but the man kicked a foot down into his chest, forcing Teddy down onto the rubble. Sharp corners of debris cut into his back. Teddy gritted his teeth, desperate not to scream. The man pressed down onto Teddy's chest and the pressure became too much. Teddy's eye bulged and it felt like he was about to split at the seams. The pain was worse than anything he'd ever felt, increasing as the man pressed harder and harder and he closed his eye to try and block out the pain. As his left side split open, Teddy screamed. Bunches of off-white fluff spilt out onto the cold floor and his vision tunneled.

From a dark alley to Teddy's right came several voices. They spoke in quiet voices, discussing inaudibly a conversation that seemed far removed from the frantic, horror-filled conversations common to this place, as if they were lovers from a time long ago past, talking as if there wasn't a care in the world.

The man glanced at the approaching couple, back down at Teddy, then back at the couple. He swore, then rose to his knees and fled just as the couple turned the corner.

Panting, Teddy crawled towards the concrete pipe, his vision tunnelling.

He heard Amira sob, then the dark night

swallowed him.

***

A bright light seared Teddy's eye. His mind wandered as he tried to think. Was he in heaven? Had he died, having finally met his match? Or, was he somehow back at Amira's parents' house? Had the past year been a dream? Perhaps this was a spell by one of the demons that lurked inside Amira's bedroom wardrobe. *Yes*, Teddy thought, *I must have succumbed to a terrible enchantment. There's no way this past year was real.*

Teddy allowed the warming brightness to wash over him as he assessed his body. His cuts had been sown together. His muscles ached, feeling like he'd fought for a week without stopping. However, inside him, the fire still smoldered. His purpose, his calling, was still as strong as ever.

"She's malnourished," a male voice said. "We need to give her some food and water."

"Let her sleep,' the female responded. 'We'll feed her when she wakes."

Teddy shifted and opened his eye. This couldn't be a dream -- how could a demon know about malnourishment? He took in his surroundings. He was in a living room and had been laid down on a table next to two chipped china cups and a pot of tea. Two paintings hung on the wall he could see, one a painting of a white city built into a mountain, standing tall and majestic in the sunlight, a white banner blowing in the wind; the other a large lake spreading out towards a tall and sprawling castle. Tension left him. This part of the city mustn't have been affected by the war yet.

The war.

It had changed everything. No longer would he need to protect Amira from the dangers of her vivid imagination -- he had to protect her from real dangers. A desperate man down a dark alley, the hungry who sought to take everything from her. Amira's need for his protection had changed him, too: he'd become stronger, more alert. His ability to sense danger had increased each night that Amira had lived on the streets. From the moment Amira had carried him from the destroyed residential block, Teddy's purpose had changed entirely.

Amira's moving on, he thought, his inner voice calm and reassuring. *There's nothing you can do now. She needs real help, the kind you can't provide anymore. You have done enough. You have saved her.*

Teddy's mind went blank and warmth spread through him. For the first time in many months he felt relaxed, as if all of his cares in the world had simply gone away. Peace had come at last.

Something stirred nearby jolting Teddy back to the present. The man and women knelt beside the threadbare sofa on which Amira lay, her small, frail body covered by an off-white blanket.

Teddy moved himself forward an inch, wincing at the pain in his side. He didn't care about the pain or being seen, he had to be by Amira's side. He tried to sit up, to look for his sword. His head started to swim again.

No, Teddy thought. *I've got to protect her.*

"Amira," he whispered.

Teddy had never spoken to her before. It had never felt right to make her aware of who he really was - her guardian angel, an agent of the night tasked with protecting her from all things dangerous and scary. To announce his existence felt wrong, taboo almost. But something within Teddy knew what the sensations meant: his role as Amira's protector was coming to an end.

Her world is no longer filled with demons inside wardrobes or octopuses trying to pull her underwater, the calming voice in his head said.

Teddy pushed himself up slightly and caught sight of his body. His golden knees were scruffy, parts of the inner fluff visible beneath his skin. The golden fur on his elbows was wearing thin, his body was riddled with other scuffs and scars. War-torn, Teddy suddenly felt old and frail, a teddy of his years. The smoldering fire faltered.

Had he done enough? He'd watched over Amira since he'd arrived at her home, a gift from loving parents for their beautiful baby girl. He'd kept his beady black eyes on the doors in her bedroom, peered under the bed several times a night to make sure nothing was going to crawl out and get her. He had fought the black octopus, kept the terrible wardrobe demons at bay, fighting where required to keep Amira's hearth and home safe and secure. And when the war had come, he'd tried his best to keep her from harm. Yes, there had been things he couldn't protect her from -- the hunger, the thirst and the cold, her need for her parents' protection -- but he'd done his best. Hadn't he?

It wasn't enough, a critical voice inside his head told him. *It was never enough.*

Amira stirred. Teddy slumped to his side and turned to look at her, tears forming in his one good eye. Her dark hair was matted with dirt, her brown skin covered in dust from the street. Amira pulled the blanket around her shoulders and fell back into sleep. Teddy felt a pang of jealousy -- Amira used to reach out for him when she was asleep.

"She's had a hard few months, I think," the man said, rubbing his hands through his balding hair. He picked up a cup of tea from the table. Though young, his face was creased with worry, but there was an affectionate look in his eyes.

"She'll be fine," the woman said, taking a seat beside the man. She rested her head on the man's shoulder. "We can help her."

Teddy's vision blurred and a dark, heavy fog descended on his mind. Between the wisps of swirling black fog, the calming voice called softly to him. *You've done enough...let her go.* He tried to struggle against it, but the fog was too thick, the warmth too comforting.

Perhaps it is time, Teddy thought. The warming darkness crept through Teddy's legs and up his body. He felt weightless, like he was being held by the entire universe. He looked towards Amira, now a dark grey shape behind the grey mists of Teddy's tired mind, and pride swelled within him. *I've done enough,* he thought. *I love you...* Teddy's eye closed and his body went limp.

Amira shifted in her sleep, a frown forming on her soft, resting face.

"Teddy?" she mumbled.

The man looked over at the scruffy golden teddy. He put down his cup and reached over to the small golden lifeless bear. He picked it up gently and placed it in Amira's arms. She pulled Teddy towards her, her frown easing into a gentle smile.

Teddy's eye opened. He turned to look up at Amira, now deep in sleep, and his chest swelled with pleasure and he grinned from ear to ear.

what secrets
Lee Clark Zumpe

what secrets will be found
amidst the spiral structure of our galaxy
by the great explorers of future generations?

what exoplanets will be discovered
across the Scutum-Centaurus and
    Perseus arms,
brimming with stars young and old?

what alien artifacts will be recovered
as humanity's reach extends beyond
    the solar system,
exploring the universe with new
    technologies?

what worlds will be terraformed,
what planets colonized and tamed,
what distant shore will become a
    far-flung paradise?

what will our distant descendants
    remember?
what recollections will that future diaspora
    keep
to connect them to their ancestral home?

Ants from Space
Bruno Lowagie

"How much does this spaceship cost?" Michael inquires.

"Doesn't it have a price tag?" the man behind the counter replies.

"If it has, I can't find it," Michael persists.

"Let me take a look at it."

The man takes the toy from the boy and examines it closely. To his surprise, the object doesn't look familiar. He has never seen it in his store, nor in the catalog from which he orders his merchandise twice a year. A white lie won't hurt the boy, he thinks, so he answers: "Ah, now I understand! It's one of the toys from our old stock. I could have sworn we sold them all out. Well, you can have it for a steal at twenty dollars."

Michael produces a twenty-dollar note from his pocket and places it on the counter. The man puts the money in his cash register and the spaceship in a bag.

***

"What's happening?" Captain Mier asks as he enters the bridge of the spaceship. "I was about to have lunch when everything started shaking."

"A boy discovered our hiding place on the top shelf of the toy store," Lieutenant Fourmi answers. "He just bought us for twenty dollars."

"Does he know this is a real spaceship crewed by ants?"

"I doubt it," the lieutenant replies. "He thinks we're a toy."

"Show me a visual, Sergeant Ameise," the captain commands.

"Aye, aye, Captain!" the communications officer replies.

She manipulates a few buttons on her desk. The large screen at the front of the bridge shows the situation around the ship from different camera angles.

"Enlarge the image on camera five," the captain says. "I believe we're attached to the luggage rack of a bicycle. The boy is probably driving us to his house."

The captain is right. Michael stops at his house, takes the spaceship under his arm, and runs to his room.

"He's putting us on his bed, Captain," the lieutenant says. "We'll make a soft landing."

"Unfortunately, we don't know what he plans to do with us," Captain Mier worries. "We must prevent him from causing additional damage to our ship. Can we project a message on the ceiling of his room?"

"I'm working on it," Sergeant Ameise answers.

***

Michael can't wait to show his best friend the cool new toy he bought. He leaves the spaceship on his bed and runs outside to tell Jake, the boy next door.

"What does it do?" Jake asks impatiently. "Can it make sounds? Does it have lights? Can it shoot projectiles?"

"I don't know," Michael answers, dragging his friend to his room. "The spaceship didn't come with a manual. It wasn't even in a box."

"Wow," Jake says as he enters Michael's room. "It can project words onto the ceiling!"

"Oioioioi Oi Oiapoioi Oiapoioi Apapap," Michael reads out loud.

"What does that mean?" Jake asks.

"I have no idea," Michael replies. He clearly doesn't understand the language of ants, which is very similar to Morse code. He grabs the spaceship from his bed and gives it a good shake.

"Don't do that!" Jake warns him. "You'll break it."

***

"Make it stop!" Captain Mier shouts as he is almost thrown out of his command chair. "Lieutenant Fourmi, do we have a torpedo at the ready?"

"We have four torpedoes ready to fire, Captain," the lieutenant yells back.

"Let's fire one, but be careful not to hit the children," the captain orders.

"Understood, Captain," the lieutenant replies. "I'll try not to hurt anyone."

He presses a button, and a torpedo accidentally hits Michael's school project. The glass of the ant farm explodes. Shards, dirt, and ants fly all over the boy's desk.

***

"Oops, what have I done?" Michael gasps.

"Cool!" Jake cheers. "You probably pressed a button to shoot a bullet."

"I didn't do anything," Michael pouts. "The spaceship did that by itself, and now my ants are escaping from their farm! I'll flunk my biology class."

"Is that the excuse you're going to tell your mother?" Jake asks, laughing.

Michael doesn't reply. He puts the spaceship back on his bed and looks at the damage the toy's torpedo has caused.

***

"They have left the room, Captain," Lieutenant Fourmi reports, "but the torpedo made an involuntary direct hit. It freed a colony of ants from some kind of prison."

"Can we communicate with the escaped prisoners?" the captain asks.

"There's only one way to find out," Sergeant Ameise replies. "I'll project a new message on the ceiling."

"I think they understand us," Lieutenant Fourmi reports. "They are marching toward us at full pace."

"Open the hatch," the captain orders. "We have to let them in before the boys come back!"

***

"What a mess!" Michael's mother sighs. "I'll clean it up on one condition; you boys need to play somewhere else while I'm busy."

"Hey, all the ants have disappeared," Jake exclaims in amazement.

"Where have they gone?" Michael trembles. "Mom, can I spend the night at Jake's house? I don't want to sleep in a room full of stray bugs tonight."

"If it's OK for Mrs. Malone, then it's also OK for me," Michael's mother replies.

"Come on, Jake," Michael urges his friend. "Let's go to your house!"

"Okay, but let's take your spaceship with us!"

***

"We're on the move again, Captain," the communications officer reports.

"You don't have to tell us, Sergeant Ameise," Lieutenant Fourmi replies, clinging to his chair. "We can all feel it."

"I hope the newcomers don't mind being shaken," the captain says. "What is their status?"

"Their leader has informed us that all the ants from his colony are safe and sound on board, Captain," Sergeant Ameise reports. "He wants to meet you and personally thank you for liberating his people."

"I want to meet him too," the captain smiles. "We're going to need him if we ever want to get off this planet."

***

Michael and Jake play with the fantastic toy all afternoon, but they are disappointed as it no longer produces special effects. They have no idea that the ship has a real crew, much less that all aboard are praying to the Great Ant. The ants beg Him to make the boys stop shaking the spaceship as quickly as possible. Not a moment too soon, Mr. Malone comes to the rescue when he calls the boys to the table: "Dinner time!"

Michael and Jake wash their hands and join the rest of the Malone family for dinner. They leave the spaceship in the playroom.

***

"It looks like all the humans are gone, Captain," Lieutenant Fourmi reports.

"Finally!" Captain Mier sighs in relief. "Time to take action."

He has discussed the plan several times with the colony leader. The leader has assigned his working ants to three different units.

One unit explores the kitchen to gather sugar crystals, the fuel the spacecraft needs to fly. Captain Mier and his crew had to carry out an emergency landing on Earth because their ship had run out of glucose. Another unit collects tools and spare parts in Mr. Malone's garage. Finally, a third unit repairs the damage the ship sustained during landing. Each unit carries out its task with military discipline.

"The ship is almost repaired, Captain Mier," the colony leader says upon sunrise. He is proud of what his colony has achieved.

"It's almost time to say goodbye," the captain replies gratefully. "My proposal still stands. We welcome you and your group to join us on our journey through space."

"Thank you for this nice offer, Captain, but I'm afraid we'd rather stay on Earth," says the colony leader. "We're not the traveling kind."

"I understand," the captain nods. "I thank you for everything you have done for us. I just want to ask you one last favor."

***

The next morning, Jake and Michael can no longer find the spaceship anywhere.

"It can't have flown away by itself, can it?" Mrs. Malone says. She doesn't know how wrong she is.

Michael returns home to sulk in his room, but his mood immediately lightens up when he finds a surprise on his pillow. He hurries back to his best friend: "Jake, I found a twenty-dollar note on my bed. Let's go to the toy store and buy another fun toy to play with!"

***

"Mission accomplished," the colony leader says when he sees the boys leave the house. At Captain Mier's request, an elite team of his best soldiers broke into the toy store early in the morning. The commando stole back the ill-gotten money that Michael paid for the spaceship.

The colony leader looks at the blue sky and tries to imagine what new adventures await his alien friends. He knows the ants from space can't hear him anymore, but he salutes them anyway: "Live long and prosper!"

Blue Marble
Nicholas Samuel Stember

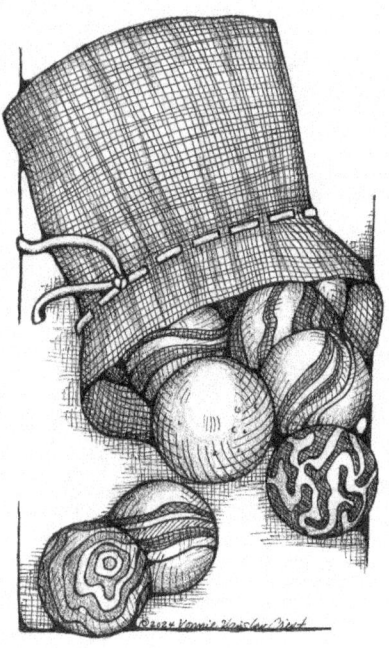

Blue Marble by Vonnie Winslow Crist

"We're playing for keeps today," Aiden said with a smile that held just a touch of cruelty to it.

Juan stared at all the marbles that were already in the large playing circle that was outlined in the dirt of the playground, ten of which were contributed by him. Seven of them were cat's eyes which were very common, clear with a swash of color in the center, he had lots of them, two of them were swirls, an opaque mixture of white and blue swirled together. He liked them more than the cat's eyes, but his attention was fixed on his purie, a clear glass marble of deep sparkling blue.

The blue marble was his favorite of all his marbles for it had been given to him by his late father, and it was special in ways he really couldn't describe, even if he had put his young voice into saying it out loud. It was special, that's all he needed to know. Not only that, but it also gave him luck in the game, and he was always sure to knock it out first.

The more he stared at it, the worse the lump in his throat grew. Aiden wasn't the best marbles player on the playground, but at twelve he was the biggest kid there, and he often let his size settle anything he didn't like. Juan quickly pulled another cat's eye out of his bag of marbles and went to replace the purie.

"Not happening," Aiden quickly swatted Juan's hand away harder than he had to. "All the game marbles are set."

"We never play for keeps!" Mari said as she looked at Juan's hurt expression and then glared at Aiden. At ten, she was a year older than Juan and often stood up for him.

"My game, my rules," the older boy said with a sneer.

"Then we're not playing," Mari said with determination as she started to reach for both of their marbles, but aiming for Juan's purie first, knowing how much it meant to her friend.

But Aiden took a stand over the marble circle and blocked her. "We rotate who picks the game, and it's finally my turn...and this time we're playing for keeps. You can quit if you like, but the marbles stay."

There were three other kids in the circle, ranging from seven to nine, but none said a word, despite the feeling of unease. None of them wanted to lose their marbles but all were afraid to stand up to Aiden.

Mari looked around for an adult but wasn't sure if any of them would actually take a side here as both of them had come on their own, as they did almost every Saturday. Their parents were fine with this as the park was fenced in with a guard and considered quite safe.

"It will be OK," Juan said to his best friend, knowing if he didn't say anything that

Mari would continue to press the point and he had no doubts Aiden wouldn't balk at hitting a girl.

"But your blue marble," she whispered to Juan, but not quietly enough.

"Oh, that's as good as mine," Aiden said with harsh chuckle.

Juan's face scrunched up. "Then I go first," he declared, determined to get his blue marble out of harm's way.

"Nuh-uh," Aiden said. "My turn to pick the game, I go first."

Juan looked longingly at his blue purie and noted it was almost in the dead center of the ring, certainly not an easy early target to knock out of the ring. "Ok," he finally agreed as he felt Mari take his hand as she sat back down.

"I'll try to get it too," she assured him. "That way our chances double of you keeping it."

Juan looked around the circle to see when his turn would be coming. Aiden was going first, and they always went counterclockwise, that put two other kids between them meaning he would be going fourth.

Typically, the lead player would go hard at the center of the pack of marbles, trying to scatter them and getting as many out of the circle as possible, as long as he got even one to go out, he'd get to go again. Juan once saw Aiden win a game without ever letting another kid play and that memory made his stomach hurt.

Aiden's shooter was a big black aggie that he used every time, and he lined up his shot and Juan could see he wasn't just aiming for the dead center, but specifically his blue purie. With a flick of his thumb the large black marble shot out of his hand and raced directly at its target, striking the blue marble with a loud 'clack' and sending it flying off towards the edge of the circle.

Juan felt his breath catch in his throat as he watched his precious marble head out with enough speed to easily clear the edge of the circle...but it didn't. It stopped abruptly an inch from the edge like it had struck an invisible wall.

Juan continued to hold his breath as all the other kids stared in disbelief, especially Aiden. They had been careful, as always, when preparing the circle to make sure the dirt was even and flat and without divots and stray gravel or stones that would interfere with the game, but Aiden instantly reached over and lifted the blue purie and stared at the dirt where it had stopped. There was nothing to block its path.

"Put it back," Mari said defiantly as she really wasn't afraid of the older boy. "It didn't go out, so put it back."

Aiden reluctantly put the marble back where it had stopped. "Fine," he said, obviously not happy with the results, leaving his black shooter where it had stopped.

The next kid looked at the blue purie and noted how close it was to the edge, an easy target, but then he looked up at Juan and smiled. He took out his shooter and went for a different group of marbles and managed to knock two out. He claimed both and shot again but didn't score again so his turn was over.

The third kid also glanced up at Juan, but smiled sheepishly and said, "Sorry, gotta try for it Juan, it's just too easy."

He aimed for the blue marble and his large aggie zoomed across the dirt and struck the blue marble but seemed to skip over it and bounced out of the circle, leaving the blue marble where it was, but not before striking two other marbles that move directly between the blue purie and where Juan was sitting.

"That's weird," Aiden said with a scowl and picked up the blue marble again, looking for any imperfections in the small sphere.

"Stuff happens," Mari said. "It's Juan's turn now so put it back."

Again, Aiden reluctantly placed the marble back down where it was.

Juan lined up for the shot, but it was not an easy one, his best bet was to hit one of the marbles in the way and make it knock his blue one out. He lined up the shot with his opaque white aggie and flicked it out with his thumb. His aim was good, but the marble in the way didn't head off on the correct angle and missed his blue one. Not only that, but he also didn't score any marbles, so his turn was over.

Mari tried as well, got one of the obstructing marbles out of the way and got to go a second time, but missed completely.

The last kid scored a few marbles close to her but didn't seem interested in Juan's blue marble as it was on the opposite side of the circle from her.

Aiden grinned as his turn came back up. "Say goodbye to your precious purie."

He lined up the shot again, and Juan started to feel horrible, but then a calming sensation started to come over him. He remembered how when he was younger and feeling upset, his father would lift him up high and put him on his shoulders and let him stay there for a while as they walked around. On top of his dad's shoulders, nothing could go wrong, and that was the feeling that wrapped around Juan like a blanket, and he smiled.

"You won't be smiling soon," Aiden said, then let the shot fly. Once again, his black aggie streaked across the dirt at the blue marble and it looked like the aim was perfect, but it wasn't. His shooter first hit another marble, knocking it out of the circle and then struck the blue marble on the far side, knocking it a few inches further back into the circle. Aiden's face got a bit red as he picked up the marble he had just won and repositioned himself to shoot again from where his aggie lay, aiming directly for the blue marble. The shot hit the marble squarely and again the blue marble streaked across the dirt, but then began to curve, almost as if the dirt circle was really a bowl, getting close to the edge but never touching the line, just rolling around the edge.

"What the hell, Juan," Aiden accused. "You put in some weighted marble?"

Mari picked up the blue purie and rolled it along the dirt, it went straight and smoothly to rest a few feet from where she rolled it. Then she picked it up and put it back in the circle where it had stopped.

"Maybe you just stink at this game," she said with a smile.

Juan flinched internally. He really admired Mari's bravery but didn't trust Aiden. When Aiden's face got even redder and he started to get up, Juan pointed at the various adults around in the park. "Hurt her and I'll yell."

Aiden looked like he was going to snap at him, but instead turned to the two kids that were next up. "Get that blue marble out of the circle for me and I'll let you have three of my marbles from after this game, any choice but my black shooter."

This time neither of the two kids hesitated and both aimed at the purie. The first hit it well enough but it just continued around the circle, still curving like it was in a bowl. The second kid's shooter was much closer, and he gave it his best shot, but all it did was continue to roll the blue marble until it was right in front of where Juan was sitting.

Juan smiled and said, "Thanks papá." Then he easily reached around the blue marble and tapped it across the line with his aggie. He picked up the blue marble and held it in his hands for a few moments, feeling its warmth, then placed it in his bag and closed it.

"I don't think I want to play with you anymore, Aiden," Juan said.

Aiden's face contorted with anger, then he forced a nasty smile. "Then you forfeit the rest of your marbles."

"I don't care," Juan admitted. "I got back the one that really matters."

"My turn," Mari quickly cut in as she aimed her purple aggie and flicked it hard... harder than they expected her to. It shot past all the other marbles, but that wasn't her target, as she struck Aiden's black aggie hard. Knocking out a fellow shooter is not the easiest task, but she hit it strongly and it rolled towards the edge. Slower and slower looking like it would stop any moment, but just when it looked as if it had lost momentum, it suddenly picked up speed again, as if something tapped it again, and it rolled over the line of the circle.

Aiden's face went white.

"You lose, loser," Mari said with a grin as she scooped up his famous marble champion aggie.

Aiden's bottom lip fell open as he just stared at the young girl, his face an almost indescribable mixture of emotions.

"I don't want to play for keeps anymore," the girl to Mari's right suddenly said, emboldened by Aiden being ousted from the game.

"Same," agreed the others.

"Everyone, take back your own marbles," Mari instructed. "Next Saturday we play for fair, no keeps, like we usually do."

"Do I get back my marbles too?" Aiden said as he watched the other kids picking up what was theirs, his voice had lost all its bravado.

"I suppose," Mari agreed.

"Even my black aggie?" he added, his voice suddenly much younger.

Mari stared at Aiden for a moment, then looked over at Juan. "What do you think?"

"You won it from him," Juan said, "it's got to be up to you."

Mari and Juan exchanged a smile, then she turned back to the older boy. "OK, but only if there is no more pushing us around. You want to play with us, you play fair, no keeps."

Aiden seemed to think about it for a moment, then nodded sheepishly.

Mari tossed the large black marble back to him, and the older boy actually smiled.

"I feel like ice cream," Juan said as he took Mari's hand and they started to head out of the playground.

"Me too," she agreed. "You OK, Juan?"

"Today," the young boy said with a smile, "I feel like I'm riding on my papá's shoulders."

Who?

Kat Heckenbach graduated from the University of Tampa with a bachelor's degree in biology, went on to teach math, and then homeschooled her son and daughter while writing and making sci-fi/fantasy art. Now that both kids have graduated, her writing and art time is constantly interrupted by her 90 lb. boxer mix. She sells prints and original art on Etsy at www.JumpingRails.etsy.com. Enter her world at www.katheckenbach.com.

Vonnie Winslow Crist is the award-winning author/illustrator of "Shivers, Scares, and Goosebumps," "Beneath Raven's Wing," "Dragon Rain," "The Enchanted Dagger," "Owl Light," "The Greener Forest," "Leprechaun Cake & Other Tales," and other books. Her fantastical stories, poems, and art are published in Australia, Japan, India,

Italy, Spain, Germany, Finland, Canada, the UK and USA. For more info: http://www.vonniewinslowcrist.com

In 2016 **Melva Gifford** won first place in the Utah Arts Council for an MG book, Operation: Middle School Madness. Up to 2023, she gained about twelve honorable mentions and three silver honorable mentions from the Writers of the Future contest. Melva has a story, Forfeit, featured in the Jan 2021 issue of *Cricket Magazine*. She is also an oral storyteller and performs at multiple venues throughout the year.

Michael D. Winkle was born and raised in northeastern Oklahoma, eventually receiving a BA in English from Oklahoma State University. He has worked in library, bookkeeper, and data entry positions as well as "writer experience" jobs ranging from car washer to postal worker. He has had thirty short stories and one non-fiction book (*I Heard of That Somewhere*, American Hauntings Ink) professionally published, and he has started uploading longer works onto Amazon Kindle. Random favorite things: Color – teal (once called "green-blue"); Song – "Radar Love" (by Golden Earring); Poem – "The Pied Piper of Hamelin" by Browning; Author – Andre Norton; Animal – Gray Wolf; short story – "The Fog-Horn" by Ray Bradbury.

Kevin Hopson's work has appeared in a variety of anthologies, magazines, and e-zines, and he enjoys writing in multiple genres. You can learn more about Kevin by visiting his website at http://www.kmhopson.com.

Pamela Love was born in New Jersey, and worked as a teacher and in marketing before becoming a writer. Her work has appeared in various children's publications, including Spaceports & Spidersilk, Cricket, and Highlights for Children, among others. She is a member of the SCBWI, and won that organization's 2020 Magazine Merit Fiction Award for "The Fog Test", which appeared in Cricket. She lives in Maryland.

British writer **Chris Farmer** is an avid lover of fantasy and science fiction and can often be found spending time in one fictional universe or another. In this universe, when he's not working, he can be found playing video games or going on long walks, imagining that he can see Ents in the woodlands or galaxy-spanning wars in the stars. When writing, Chris likes to explore all the things that make us human. With fantastical elements, of course.

Bruno Lowagie lives and works in Ghent, Belgium. A former open-source developer and entrepreneur, he started a writing career after selling his business. Initially writing for

Dutch and Flemish audiences, he has recently begun translating his work into English.

Born in New York City, **Nicholas Samuel Stember** has lived in Europe and Israel but spent most of his life in the suburbs of Princeton, NJ. Growing up with a profound love and appreciation of the genres of fantasy, science fiction and horror, the direction his writing took was firmly set. His love of those genres also found him a wife from across the sea, and he ended up marrying her and moving to the Faroe Islands, where he resides today in a four generation house.

Lauren McBride finds inspiration in faith, family, nature, science, and membership in the SFPA. Nominated for the Best of the Net, Pushcart, Rhysling, and Dwarf Stars Awards, her poetry has appeared internationally in speculative and mainstream publications including Asimov's, Fantasy & Science Fiction, and Utopia Science Fiction's 5th Anniversary Anthology. Her chapbook, Aliens, Magic, and Monsters, was published by Hiraeth (2023). She enjoys swimming, gardening, baking, reading, writing, and knitting scarves for U.S. troops.

Jay Sturner is a poet, fiction writer, and naturalist from the Chicago suburbs. He is the author of several books of poetry and a collection of short stories. His writing has appeared in such publications as The Magazine of Fantasy & Science Fiction, Space & Time, and Star*Line, among others. He mainly writes fantasy, horror, and science fiction, but occasionally writes in other genres. Sturner is also a professional birdwalk leader and former botanist.

Denise Noe is author of "The Bloodied and the Broken," "Justice Gone Haywire," "I Spy, You Spy, They Spy," "A Sheep in Wolf's Clothing: The Life of Marie Windsor," and "Ayn Rand at the Movies." Her Instagram has over 90K followers. https://www.youtube.com/channel/UCFFDe5wl9-C6T8CagiRnEaA/videos
https://www.instagram.com/denisenoe1957/

Lisa Timpf's speculative poetry has appeared in a variety of magazines and anthologies, including New Myths, Star*Line, Eye to the Telescope, Liquid Imagination, and Polar Borealis. When not writing, Lisa enjoys organic gardening, bird-watching, and walking her lively Jack Russel-cocker spaniel Chet. You can find out more about Lisa's writing at http://lisatimpf.blogspot.com/.

Lee Clark Zumpe, an entertainment editor with Tampa Bay Newspapers, earned his degree in English at the University of South Florida. He began writing poetry and fiction in the early 1990s. His work has regularly appeared in a variety of literary journals and genre magazines over the last two decades. Publication credits include *Tiferet*, *Zillah*, *The Ugly Tree*, *Modern Drunkard Magazine*, *Red Owl*, *Jones Av.*, *Main Street Rag*, *Space & Time*, *Mythic Delirium* and *Weird Tales*.

Lee lives on the west coast of Florida with his wife and daughter.

www.ingramcontent.com/pod-product-compliance
Lightning Source LLC
LaVergne TN
LVHW012031060526
838201LV00061B/4557